The Mysterious Haunted Castle

Written By   Boutaina Achi

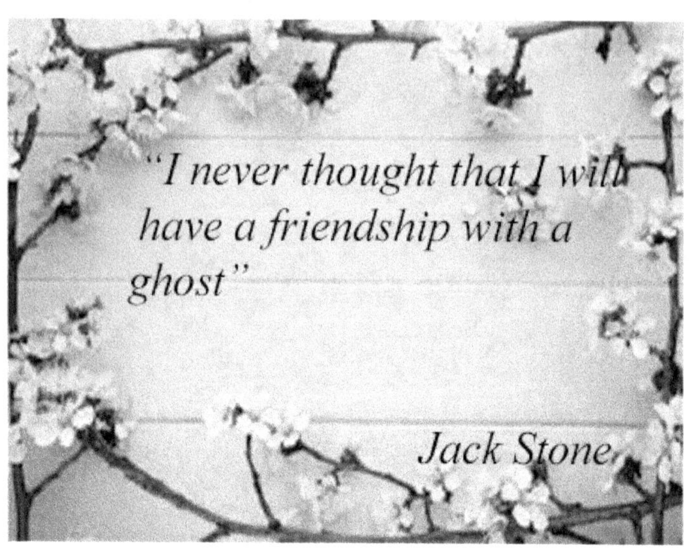

Introduction

This story is based on Actual events, My grandmother used to tell us stories in childhood this is one of the stories that I've been touched With Some of the events are from my imagination but unfortunately, I have nothing that can document it, The main character in this story tells that he was in a friendship with a ghost that suffers in a very long time, I personally believe in that because I experienced some events in my childhood as supernatural events, I HOPE YOU ENJOY THE STORY REGARDLESS MY ENGLISH.

The Mysterious House

Once upon a time , there was a rich   man ,looking for a quiet place to live in, he didn't find better than the countryside regions. After a long travel he finally found his destination, Amazing views, full of colorful flowers, huge fields ,simple people with simple clothes, old style buildings, between all of these things, this man only attracted by an old century castle, no doubts, the castle looks something interesting and precious, the man wants to know the castle's story, a castle like that must have an interesting story, he started to ask people there but everyone ignored him with the fear looks in their faces ,except an old man was listening to him,he told him that there are a lot of stories and rumors about the castle one of the famous rumor was, it was belong to a Royal family everyone was happy to live there because the Royal family was so kind to everyone, several dynasties were lasted to take the authority after them but nobody knows what happened after .A long time after, a foreign lady attracted by the castle and she bought it with extra happiness , she was impressed with all of the precious decorations and the amazing portraits ,she was really in love with the design of everything in it, she spent a calm, fresh morning in the garden .

After the whole normal day, sunset had arrived, the lady went to sleep, suddenly, a hard childish screaming made her up, she went to check out to whom it belongs, she found a scary ghost floating here and there, after this scary night , she left in early morning, saying to people what happened to her, until now no one have been brave to buy or even could take a look on it. The man thanked the old man for the story, but he had some doubts about this rumor and some faith too. Even though he decided to buy the castle and find out what's really happened in that castle a long ago!!!!

The Rich man started to look around the town to get close to people in there and why not makes friendships with, the people seems polite and so welcoming, everyone looks so loyal to his own job, he kept looking and he saw that the town had a lot of fields, it is an agricultural blooming area, except the field by the castle. the land is dead like a desert, what's push the man and made him so excited to find out the secret of the castle and to find who's the screaming belongs to, he came closer to the field and found some old toys and old children books.....

The Closer Look

The man get closer to the field by the castle and he found some old toys and old children books, he looked around to make sure that there is no one in the area, he decided to enter to the castle, moved step by step until got to a huge showy door, heart beats getting fast and faster, the door opened with a noisy sound, the Man stunned on what he looked at, " so Amazing! ", He said, After all these years the castle looked so clean, and all the old castle equipments still there, he looked around impressed with the decoration of the castle, portraits everywhere, statues, walls paintings, even the roses in the vases are bloomy," *How the roses are opened like if someone irrigate them everyday!"*. He said.

The Man could not stop staring at the beauty and the mystery covered the building, he went out to the garden, he was so fascinated with the work there, all the kinds of roses and flowers are there and they were very well cared, he took a couple of hours amusing his eyes with the beautiful views and got relaxed hearing birds tweets. The man finished his journey in the castle. he went out to buy what he needs for dinner, he came back to "home" and made a delicious dinner, turned on the fire and started to eat slowly, enjoying his dinner with the fire's sound coming from the chimney. After dinner, he went to the library, a very large library, it contained variety of books, he found an old book named "The Royal family history", he took a seat, ignited the candles and started reading carefully until something dropped down from the book , it was a picture, an old picture of a little pretty girl, he felt weird, while he was looking at the picture suddenly hard knocks on the door cut this feeling, he went to open the door while wondering who's knocking on this time of night, he is still new here and doesn't know anyone well,"*Oh! it's you!, I was just crossing by, until I saw the lights from the window, can I come in?"*. said the neighbour.

The man: yes, sure.

The neighbour: thanks.

The man: come and have a seat.

They continued their talk while drinking coffee.

The neighbour: May I ask you a question?

The man: yes, of course go ahead.

The neighbour: did you buy the castle?

The man: No, but I'm thinking of it, but for the moment I just want to know how living here looks like.

The neighbour: do you know its story.

The man: yes, an old man told me about it.

The neighbour: are you sure that you want to live here?

The man: yes, I did not find it a problem.

The neighbour: Actually, it looks so comfortable, but I'm not brave to stay longer, Anyway, I'll take my way now, thank you for the coffee and for the nice chat, please be careful!

The man: thank you for your concern, but I still want to live here and find the true story of this place.

The neighbour: okay, Good night.

The man: get safe, Good night.

Jack Stone

Buying The Castle

It gets late the man feels so sleepy, he got upstairs, chose one of the bedrooms there and he lay on the bed, thought of the neighbour's talk and of the mystery book until he slept, A very beautiful view.... a little girl running happily, laughing so hard in the field until she got to the bridge, she turned around, looked at the man with a smiley face called his name so hard (Jaccckkk, HELP!!), and jumped from the bridge. Three Am ,Jack woke up shocked from what the girl did *"Ohh, it was just a dream, I felt like it's real"*, he could not return to sleep, he got up and turned around in the room wondering *"who is this girl, it looks so familiar but i could not organizer her? and how she knew my name?"*

Jack stayed awake until the morning , he is now more excited about the castle than before, he got downstairs, He had his breakfast in the garden ,while having his meal, he decided to buy the castle to find out the relation between the castle and the little girl. The man had been isolated from people for a while; he was busy

with discovering the castle. He went out to announce to people that he bought the castle.

When he got out ,he met his neighbour .

The neighbour: Good morning Jack!

Jack: Good morning!

The neighbour: I was so worried about you, you've been absent for a while?

Jack: thank you for your concern, I am very well and everything is okay.

The neighbour :Ohh , yeah?, great to hear that, so you did buy the house .

Jack: yes, I did.

group of women were listening to their talk .

The woman: Oh, sorry young man, but what did I hear is true ?did you buy the castle?

Jack: yes, what you heard is right...

The woman: Ohh! is something weird happened to you in your first days there?

Jack: Well, No, nothing happened but I did feel something weird about that place, weird in a good way, so that's why I decided to buy it.

The woman: I think what happened to the lady at that time was only a rumor.

The neighbour: nobody knows , we can't confirm that, but we have Jack , who can do it.

Jack: yes that's right .

The neighbour: I already warned you, and I'll say it again beware from such a place .

Jack: Thank you.

The woman: such a brave man ,you are!!

Jack excused the women for a leave, they were so fascinated with his bravery and his good looking.

He started his morning's hiking, greeting people, and transfer from this neighbourhood to another, he met new people, made some friendship, he stop before a store to buy his needs and went to his new house, he felt so tired and so hungry, when he came to the castle ,he noticed that the lights are on....

Little Marie

The First Meeting

When Jack came to the castle he noticed that the lights were on, *"Maybe I forgot to switch them off "* He said. He was so hungry and so tired he couldn't make dinner for himself , he wished that some-body would do it instead of him. Jack entered the castle, a nice smell came out , he got in so fast to the kitchen, *"Oh my God ,the dinner is served , How could it be possible!!"*

He looked around, nobody was there suddenly he heard a child's voice , a little girl came out , he thought of leaving the castle im-mediately , he froze stunned.

The girl : don't freak out Jack ,I made the dinner for you, don't worry I'm not going to hurt you ,go ahead and enjoy it.

Jack:T T Thank you ,okay I'll take a seat ,*(OH!it's the girl from the picture).*

The girl: Alright, I'll leave you now.

Jack started eating with a shaking body, he could not resist the food , it looked so delicious:*"Oh my God ,I can not believe it and she made dinner for me , oh my god!"*

He finished his meal and went to the living room, he took a sit and started to think of the girl she looks so

friendly and polite *"If I see her the next time,I'll definitely try to talk to her"*. He slept and dreamed about her all night....

Five Am , Jack woke up and went to the garden to take some fresh air , he noticed like there was someone running in the field *"Oh maybe it's her , wait.... wait , I'm not going to hurt you please wait little girl"*. Jack kept running after her but he could not catch her, she ran until she get to the bridge, and stopped there looked at Jack ,After seconds she disappeared, he spent all the day in the field waiting for her to come back, he returned to home upset , but he felt a kind of happiness that he met her again without fear, he wanted to meet her again so badly and have a nice chat with her, and why not know her hidden story from her, he spent his day normally , and tried to keep what he saw in secret.

A few days passed and the girl did not show up again , Jack felt so lonely, it's like in their first meeting , the girl added something to the castle, something that he would miss so much ,he hoped that she would not go forever. Jack went to the mailbox to see if he had some lettres there , he didn't ask for his family since he came to the countryside, he found a letter from his mom:

" my dear son ,

I missed you so much , I hope that you're reached in the countryside in good health , did you find a good girl for you? If yes I will be happy to meet you and your girl at a family dinner as soon as possible , come and visit your mother in this fall".

The Girl's Absence

When Jack read his mom's letter, he got confused ,he was so happy to get a letter from her ,but he thought of the girl,what if she came in his absence? He stayed a few days in case the little girl came back . Three days passed the girl did not come back .Her absence made Jack so sad and distracted ,he isolated himself from the society, no one saw him after days,his neighbour get worried about him and he went to visit him.

The neighbour: tok tok! jackkk, are you there?

After minutes ,Jack opened the door .

The neighbour: Ohh! Look at you! you look miserable ,what happened to you my friend, I'm here for you !

Jack could not talk , stand at the neighbour and started crying .

"What happened to you? Is it because of the castle? Is something happening?" asked the neighbour.

they entered and started chatting..

Jack: nothing happened , but I'm not feeling well.

The neighbour: if you need to talk about something, I'm here.

Jack: thank you, you're a real friend , I want you to stay with me tonight.

They spent all the night talking about their lives, and laughing about their funny events.

the neighbour's talk indeed makes it up for Jack.

Six o'clock in the morning , the neighbour woke up, and prepared breakfast, Jack woke up due to the good smell that covered the house .

Jack: Good morning!

The neighbour: Good morning Jack ,I hope did not wake you .

Jack: No, you didn't, it's time for waking anyway.

They finished their meal, then they went out together, the neighbour tried his best to let Jack forget about whatever he made him living this, they spent a nice time together, but Jack did not forget in any single minute about the girl , wondering in himself *"why she didn't return?, I hope that she is fine and that she will come back soon".*

The neighbour asked him if this trip was useful, and made it up a little .

Jack: Of course , it does, I don't know what I'll do without you, thank you for staying with me in time I needed someone so badly.

The neighbour felt pleased with what jack said.

-" *any time.*" said the neighbour.

Jack thought, if he could return to the castle or not, what if the girl disappeared forever, maybe he would forget all about and get back to his city, he thought to tell his friend about it ....

Jack: My friend , can I ask you something?

The neighbour: yes, sure, anything .

Jack: Something about the castle, do you really think that ....(*take a breath*).. OK , never mind it's nothing.

The neighbour: Okay.

"No, I can't stop all of this, because of her absence, I know that she will return sooner and I will definitely know everything I need".

Jack Happy Again

Jack was grateful to his friend , and decided to return to the castle. sunset came, Jack felt so relieved after the sadness, he was no longer far from the castle, he saw lowlights coming through the castle windows, he ran so fast hoping that the girl had returned .Delicious smell coming from the kitchen,the dinner

was prepared but no one was there, he looked at the table and he saw two dishes on it, *"Oh, I can't resist the food, maybe I'll put some on my dish"* ,**(looking around, and waiting for the girl to show up).**
-*"you will start without me? what an impolite man!"*,
 he stunned, *"Oh! my apology, after you"*. responded Jack.
Jack was extremely happy because the girl is finally here , he wanted to hug her and asked about the reason of her absence but after all she is not a normal person, she is a supernatural one even if she looks innocent, he finished his meal in silence, they just look at each other, then she started smiling and said *" this is the first time that I feel comfortable with someone , you know, I felt alone for a longer time , and there you are cutting my loneliness, thank you for coming here"*.
Jack: I have the same feeling too.
The girl stood up and looked at Jack and said, *"I hope you to stay here forever"*, then she left.
Jack: Wait , wait I have to tell you something, when I can see you again?
Jack was extremely happy, and he was touched with the girl's words. He wished that he could stay forever in the castle and met that innocent girl always, he had not the chance to tell her that he must go to his city till unknown time. Jack went to his bed , he could not sleep because he was happy but kind of missed his old life, living in a big city is so much different than living in countryside, missing his family that no one talked to each other since he came there, he thought to write to his mom sooner , to not think that something happened to him or he just ignored her. Jack wanted to do something different in his left days in the countryside, he was a famous lawyer in the city he lives in , he wanted to get a new job , not for money but only to full his time .

Jack woke up, prepared his morning coffee , and went to the garden , he did not took care of the garden since he came there , because he knew that someone was taking care of it, but this time the garden was different , it was not fully of life like before , this is definitely has a relation with the girl, the lands are agricultural ones , but the field by the castle is dead like a desert what Jack noticed in the beginning , he wondered what makes this land die, why exactly this land by the castle, no doubts , the little girl is the key of its story.

The Field By The Castle

When Jack got closer to the field , he saw the girl running happily in the field , then he noticed , when the girl touched the ground the plants came to life , but when she removed her feet it died, *"Oh my God , how this could be possible".*said jack.

 Jack tried to catch the girl and ask her what's going on , but he couldn't, the girl kept running faster, she got to the bridge and started crying and screaming so hard and said : *"why you did that to me, stop hurting me ,I don't deserve to be punished",* looking in the bridge side, she was like talking to someone else then she looked at jack and said with a loud voice : *"Jackkkk, you must to do something, helppp mee"* then she jumped from the bridge, Jack could not do anything but he stands up freeze, this is the first time that he saw the girl screaming, crying and he was unable to move and do something . to whom she was talking? what's going on? he didn't see anything but obviously that she was suffering from pain, someone was hitting her?But why? what she had done maybe it is a story that happened a long time ago, and he just seen it before him .Jack thought of how he could help the girl from something invisible, there must be a way.

Every time it showed a mystery in this place .

We can consider Jack the brave character in this story, so he deserves to be the hero. Our hero needs help, so he could continue his trip in finding the full story of this place. The mystery book that he found before was not enough to find what's really happened because it has some missing pages and he only found the history of the Royal family, some information about each member there and a picture of the little girl, what jack remembered was that the little girl was not mentioned there, was not she relatively to the Royal family ? Jack took the book again, looked at the picture there are no information on it (no date , no writings , even the name was not written there) ,her clothes are the same clothes as "now" and they are for maids at that time , maybe she was a maid ,a maid in such age?,but definitely not from rich people, what makes a little girl like her play with her toys next to the bridge? is she hiding from someone ? was it the person hitting her minutes ago? Jack tried to link things between each other , He wanted to do his best to save the little girl from whatever was that "person".

Unexpected Guest

Jack wrote a letter to his mom,telling her that he will come to visit her sooner, He was so sad because he will leave the castle for a few days , maybe more , he hoped to see the little girl before he goes , he was so worried about her because she left after she was hitting by someone. Jack spent a calm, relaxing evening, no visitors , no one around , even outside was so calm …a weird calm , he felt kind of fear, he took a look from the window , he saw a dark shade floating out there , he got panic, *,"Oh my God, did what I see just now is real??, come down Jack maybe you start to imagine things, I need to have some rest"*, he went to the kitchen and prepared some relaxing drinks, maybe he could forget what he saw and have a good sleep, he went to living room he hold a book and had sit, started reading while drinking, suddenly Jack heard a hard knocking on the door, he freezed and he could not open it *," who is there?"*, nobody responded, Jack said in a shaking voice, *"who is knocking on the door?",* he opened it and did not find anyone, he was about to close the door but a black shade push it strongly, Jack pushed away, hit with the wall and passed away ,after couple of minutes he woke up , opened his eyes, and looked at a strange man sitting on the sofa, looking at him with his scary face , *"Oh! my God , what's going on ? who are you?Am I dreaming?".* wondered Jack. *"the guest"* assured jack and asked him to take a sit, because he wants to tell him something about the little girl, Jack sit down, and asked him how did he know about her, "The guest" avoid to answer the question and said :*" I only can tell you ,that little Marie suffered a lot in the past, and I heard you that morning talking and said that you can do anything to help her then I felt that you are the man who can save her , so here I am to tell you that you are the man that Marie needs".*

Jack felt so sad about what "the guest" told him, *"is that her name, little Marie, such a beautiful name, may I know about her full story".*

The guest: I can't tell you the full story that is what you must find out by yourself.

Jack: Is there anything that could guide me,

(the guest insists to be silent)

Jack: Anyway, thank you, it was a pleasure to know her name.

Jack's Decision

The guest disappeared without saying a word , Jack still had a lot of questions but he knew that the guest would not say more,so he needed to do it himself. The absence of the girl made Jack so worried ,especially when he knew about her suffering in the past.

Jack had not enough information to solve all of this, but he will do his best for the sake of the little Marie. Jack had decided the day of his return, So he spent his day organizing his stuff to get prepared for traveling . After a tiring day , jack took a nap ,zzz, people are celebrating with happiness, children are running everywhere , it is like in the same town but in a different time, like he got back on time , he saw a girl , she was the little Marie, she was celebrating with children , till a scary woman voice came out from nowhere, *"MARIEEE, how could you do it again, I did not punish you like I should , you will see dirty girl, you will see"*, Jack followed her to the castle but he only can listen to her crying *" please,I promise, this is the last time, i'm sorry, please stop you're hurting me, sob, sob"*.

-*" Marieeeee, where are you my dear , I'm jack ,I'm here for you dear"*

-*"Jack is that really you?"*.

-*"jack, jack are you okay? why are you sweating?"*.asked the neighbour's wife.

jack woke up, looking at that pretty face , who is this , such a beautiful woman *(in a low voice)*, May I know who are you?

-*" sorry, I found your door open ,I'm your friend's wife , My name is Natalie"*

Jack blushed and answered : it's okay ,yes, I'm fine , it was just a nightmare.

Natalie: you did not show up for days, I just wanted you to know if you need anything, you can just ask me . my husband had an urgency traveling ,so that's why he did not come to visit you.

Jack: I hope that is nothing bad.

Natalie: Actually yes, his father is so sick , he went to take care of him.

Jack: a soon recovery to him , you're really good people , I'm so glad to meet you.

Natalie :glad to meet you too, you are welcome.

Jack: Thank you so much for your kindness .

the neighbor's wife turned around and said , *"excuse me for being intrusive, are you going somewhere?"*

Jack: yes, I planned to visit my family in a few days.

 Natalie: Oh, the town will miss you then, have a safe trip, I let you now , have a nice day.

this is a hard decision for a man that got attached to a soul , a soul that suffered in her small age ,poor Marie ,

"I don't know how to make you come back , I wish that I could make you forget all the pain you lived in this place".

Jack went to the garden and like he expected, the garden was almost dead, even if he took care of it , the garden could not survive without little Marie.

Going Back To The City

The garden is dead with Marie's absence, even though the castle was not looking like when Marie was around , it was such a warm and comfortable place, Jack really missed that feeling .days passed and nothing had changed, jack only had the usual nightmares, and he often had seen some shades , he really was not relieved with what happened in those days.

 Six Am, jack got ready for traveling, he felt like it is a goodbye, he turned behind and took a deep look maybe the little Marie will show up, ...but she didn't, However Jack had a feeling that she was there looking at him, *"Marie, I know that you're there somewhere, believe me I will do my best to save you"*,

 he left the castle crying , when he was on his way he met Natalie and her friend.

Natalie: Good morning Jack.

Jack :Good morning ladies, what makes you wake up in such early morning, any news from your husband?

Natalie: No, he has not written since he went, I hope that he got safe there.

Jack: I'm sure he would, I want to tell you that I'm going to the train station now, if anything unusual happened in the castle , would you please write me in this address.

Natalie: Of course.

Jack left faster to not miss the train.

Natalie's friend asked her about Jack, and told her how handsome he is, she told her that he must be a crazy man.

Natalie's friend: why? I find him such a handsome gentleman.

Natalie thought that there was something else that made Jack want to travel, maybe something happened in the castle.

Natalie: Yeah, maybe, I can't Deny that he is a very brave man.

jack arrived on time to the train station.....the train moved on , Jack was so excited to visit his family after a long time, what's new there? Did things change there?

Jack was looking deep to the fields out there and amusing his eyes with the beautiful nature , he could not forget the feelings when he got out from the castle , maybe because little Marie was there for real. In a couple of hours Jack will reach his destination, Jack is used to the calm ,simple life in the countryside....after moments Jack took a nap , the trip was so long and boring, no one to talk with . After hours , Jack woke up in a noisy voice...

tickets collector man: camelotttttt , this is camelot, come on passengers!

Camelot was the destination of Jack , he get down from the train , he felt like he is new there ,as it's the first time he sees his hometown . before going to home and see his lovely parents, and his beloved siblings, he decided to go around to the city just to bring memories Jack's family is the most known in the entire city- Camelot city is such a big city- and the most elegant and noble one, his family contains his mom and dad and his two pretty sisters and three brothers .

Natalie and her friend

Marie's Sadness

Jack arrived at his home and he was so excited to meet his family, on his way home he found the guardian ," *Mister you finally here , welcome back , I'm going to tell your mom , good news like this will make her smile again"*.

Jack: No ,no I want to surprise her, what? What makes her sad is everything Alright ?

The guardian: Alright sir , you can know from her.

Jack entered and found his mom crying on the sofa....

Jack: Mom , I'm back !!

The mother: Finally my boy is here for me. How was your trip? Are you tired ? Are you hungry ? Why you did not tell me that you will come today? I would tell shoshanna to prepare your preferred dishes .

Jack: I wanted to surprise you, why you were crying? what happened and where is everyone?

The mother: I was crying because your dad is so sick, and your siblings have gone letting me here alone!

Jack: Oh my God ,where is dad? Mom don't worry everything will be alright , I'm here now.

The mother: he is upstairs, I just gave him medicine hoping for a miracle to happen. we will visit him later together, you must have A lot to tell me , did you meet any pretty girls?

Shoshannaaaa my boy is here please prepare his favorite dishes.

Shoshanna: yes, Madame.

they went to the living room, Jack told his mother about the castle he bought, the village and how people there are so kind and simple.

Jack and his mom are together now and the little Marie is floating in the castle alone, Jack was completely right, Marie was looking from the window, when he was waiting for her, but she felt so sad when she saw him leaving, little Marie considered Jack as her friend ,her saver , now she feels insecure,she wanted him to stay with her but the family comes first. Marie was in Jack's bedroom , she was looking for something belongs to him, his dairy, his books..., to feel that lost secure again...

 Natalie wondered why Jack insisted about if something happened in the castle, she got curious, she wanted to know if there is something special in there, so she decided to take a look, she find a way to throw herself from , *"Oh! my God the Garden looks horrible, was not jack taking care of the garden?, but my husband told me that the garden was fascinated, I feel uncomfortable it's better to leave this place."*

Natalie looked up, and she saw a scary face of a little girl in the window , *"Oh! God, I knew that there is something in here"* . Natalie left the castle in a hurry without telling anyone what she saw.

Shoshanna

Lady Anastasia

After eating lunch and finishing the nice chat between mom and son , Jack wanted to see his father, he went to his bedroom, he was not looking good at all ,Jack wondered if his mom was taking care of him.

To let our noble readers get familiar with the lady Anastasia, Jack's mom, Anastasia is a very educate lady ,a powerful woman, you will not be able to know if she is kind or evil , she has double character, since she got married everything was under her control , she took control of the work, the wealth ....everything she is also the castle lady ,she was hard with servers ,but everyone has weakness point or more, her weakness point is Jack ,He is completely the opposite , he is a real gentleman , She badly wanted Jack to take the whole heritage after his father's death, because his siblings are not good people at all or so she thought. Jack took a seat beside his father, his kind hearted father, and held his hand ,*" dad I hope that you can hear me, I'm Jack I just arrived from the countryside, I really missed you and want to talk to you"*.

-*"cough, cough , really is that you Jack? finally you came back to see your father before leaving"*

-*"please dad don't say that , you will live more and more"*

-*"where is Anastasia , where is she? "*

-*" she is not here , I came alone"*

-*"good, I want to tell you something, cough, cough, come closer my son , as you know, your mom doesn't like your siblings, after I'll die, definitely the heritage problems will happen and I do know that you are the only wise person in this family, So I will write to you the all heritage to die in peace, because I know that you will do the right thing"*

-*"dad please it's a big responsibility for me, what if my siblings thought that I'm the one that forced you to give me everything"*.

-*"don't worry my son, everything will be fine, I just want to die in relief"*.

Anastasia: Jack , Jack , where did you go .

Jack: I'm up here, I just wanted to put my stuff in my bedroom.

Anastasia: why you did not let Shoshanna do that for you ,honey , did you check your father?

Jack: It's okay I'll do it myself ,yes I did, but he looks like he still sleeps, So I did not want to disturb him.

Anastasia: Okay dear , you need to rest too , your trip was so long. Jack went to his bedroom and thought about his father talking and if he is really able to take this responsibility. *"I wish that innocent little girl was here with me, I feel so powerful and extremely happy when she is around, who knows what is going on with you now little Marie"*

Lady anastasia

The Shocking Truth

Marie was thinking the same while she was on jack's bed, looking at the roof, when she was alive she never dreamed to touch the door of this room because the room was belong to the Prince at that time, Marie finally felt secure again and did not get hurt for a while ,she was absolutely certain that Jack is her saver, she only stayed in his room for a couple days and "lived" in peace. In Jack's absence Marie was taking care of everything in the castle , She was so happy while she was doing it. The days had passed normally, everyone was taking care of their business, without forgetting to mention that people in the town missed Jack's presence, No wonder, he is a very kind man and people there respect him so much. Jack also missed the countryside but he has the feeling that he needs to solve other things in the city besides Marie's.

Six Am Jack woke up, went to the garden, while he was absent minded, Lady Anastasia got in....

Lady Anastasia: Good morning ,jack.

Jack: Good morning , Mom.

Lady Anastasia: I noticed that you were in deep thinking, was it your girl , hehe, come on tell your mom that you're finally deciding to have your own family, and I know that my boy will not choose any girl.

Jack: Oh! Come on mom, you know that I did not think of any girl after Helen, and I feel that something is wrong here, I can't believe that my siblings leave this house without any convincing reason.

Lady Anastasia: How many times should I say that Helen let you down, please give yourself a chance to look at the girls around, there are a lot of girls that deserve to be your wife, are you accusing your mom!!!

Jack: mom, come on, I'm just trying to know what happened.

Lady Anastasia: Okay son, it's your right, but I already told you so please, don't open this subject again.

Jack: Okay, mom I will not.

Anastasia: obedient boy, let's have our breakfast.

Anastasia is acting weird ,Obviously she is hiding something, Jack knew that he would not get his answer so he went to Shoshanna and asked her.

Jack: Good morning ,Shoshanna.

Shoshanna: Good morning ,Mister Jack.

Jack: May you tell me if something bad happened in my absence. Shoshanna started shaking right away.

Jack: take it easy.

Shoshanna: Please sir, don't make it hard for me, if the lady knows that I told you something she will kill me without any mercy .

Jack: Take it easy , dear , nothing will happen to you . **Shoshanna**: Okay, okay, when you traveled, Lady Anastasia kicked your siblings out and she was planning to kill your father , sorry sir ,I can't add more than that .

Jack: oh what? what's more than that? okay Shoshanna thank you, *(I never thought that mom could be this evil)!!* Jack went to the library for some researchers about Marie's story, Maybe he can find something in old books there and wanted to change air, what he heard from Shoshanna was horrible, he was completely shocked... standing before the library, Jack had a lot of memories about this old place, memories from college with his crazy friends .... a long time ago, when Jack was younger he was the most handsome boy in his college, he was so popular, a lot of girls have crush on him, every girl ,except one , He felt a special feeling when he looked at her in the first time....

Miss Helen

Flash Back

A very special young lady in Jack's eyes ,He quiet remember their first meeting in this old library where Jack is standing now.....A beautiful girl was taking a seat in the library with her friends around, They were preparing for the final exam....Jack entered to the library to prepare for the exam too, He took the opposite seat , put his books on the table ..... he tried to concentrate on his studies but he could not take away his eyes from the girl a front of him....the time had passed ,everyone got tired....

Veronica: Helen, I can't study more, I will go home , what about you , are you going with us ?

Helen: No, I'll stay a little bit.

Veronica: Okay dear, as you wish , but give yourself some rest.

Helen: I will , see you .

"Finally here is the chance to get to know the beautiful Helen" .said Jack

Jack thought that Maybe he can help her with her studies.

Jack: Hello ,May I take a seat ?

Helen: yes, of course the seat is empty.

Jack: Thank you .May I know which subject are you preparing?

Helen: advanced Mathematics, What about you?

Jack: I study law, I'm a fan of Maths , I can help you with it if you want to.

Helen: sure, I will not mind that, but maybe not now, it's getting late, I should go home ,Nice to meet you .....

Jack: Jack.....My name is Jack Stone, Nice to meet you too.....

Helen: I'm Helen Wolf.

A sudden silence swept the place....

Jack: Helen, such a pretty name, I think I'll go home too , May I accompany you ?

Helen: No worries ,I'll go by myself , Thank you.

Jack: you are most welcome.

he got out with Helen... The weather was on Jack's side, it rained profusely and Helen got panicked,

Jack assured her and said : the driver is waiting for me out and you will accompany me, No more words....

SIIIR How can I help you?

Such an annoying voice and an ugly face, it was the librarian lady.

Jack : Ah, yes Madam, I need a book of history of a small town named " Takshfield".

The Librarian: Okay sir, All the history books are in shelf number "22"

Jack: Thank you Ma'am.

Jack hoped to find what he was looking for ......Ohh such a big shelf contained a lot of books, He got confused , did not know where to start.

Jack found some interesting books about that town but nothing about the castle. He really needs help from a history expert but who can help him in such a story, Jack decided to continue on his own for the moment , this is only the beginning...

While Jack was busy with his research , A man entered the library and asked the librarian lady for the same thing as Jack...

About the librarian describing it was just a sense of humor, I really do like them and I appreciate their work, I really do.

Daniel Jhonson

Proposing To Helen

The man asked the librarian about a history book of the same town as Jack , she guided him to shelf number 22. The man met

Jack in a mess, he got lost in front of all those books .

The man: hello ,I'm looking for some history books, may I join you ?

Jack: Yes, sure, I really need help, I am looking for a specific history book but I did not find anything.

The man: luckily, I'm a history instructor and I'm doing research about, what book you are looking for?

Jack: Takshfield history, you?

The man: Ohh, I'm looking for the same book , what do you know about the town's history?

Jack: I don't know much however I'm interested in a castle there, it will be a pleasure if you help me about. **The man**: Of course, this is my visit card to keep in touch, I will inform you about anything new.

Jack: thank you... oh really? Is Daniel Johnson your name for real?, wow ,we had college together.

Daniel: oh yeah? May I know what your name is ?

Jack: my name is Jack stone.

Daniel: yeah , I remembered you, long time not see you my friend! How's Helen ?It seems everything is good with you glad for that , so are you two still together? **Jack**: Well , no unfortunately.

Daniel: Sorry, to hear that, but I'm really glad to finally meet you and have this short conversation.

jack: I'm glad to meet you too, such a long time, I would want to stay but I have to go.

Daniel: okay , sure my friend.

Jack got out from the library. It was a rainy day, like when he met Helen for the first time... After Jack sent Helen home , he just kept thinking about her too much, he wanted her to be his girlfriend so badly but he was afraid if she already had one.... Luckily Helen did not have a boyfriend, like she did not fill her head with those stuff.....love stuff, but the action of jack that day, let something move in Her heart. Days passed Helen and Jack became couples, even if they were still young, -university students- but this is love, you can't beat it.Jack will never break Helen's heart unless it is something out of his control.

Jack promised Helen that they would get married after graduation.It's the last college year, everyone worked hard for the final exam, and got stressed about the results. After a couple days the results came out, and everyone did well and got their diplomas, they celebrated with extra happiness, yeah really it was a hard year they deserve to celebrate their success. Jack took Helen home and he went to talk with her father. her father was waiting for her before the door, a very simple house , modest man, you can immediately feel peaceful when you are looking at his happy face. *"Welcome to our modest home"*. said Helen's father. *"thank you uncle, I want to talk with you about something, if you don't mind "*.replied Jack

Helen's dad: of course, I don't mind let's enter it's getting cold.

The uncle went to bring some coffee and cookies , Jack felt so relieved in the house , it's a very warm place.

-"welcome son once again, I just found cookies and coffee. I hope it's something you like".

Jack: Of course, there are no worries.

The uncle: First of all, I should congratulate you my kids for your graduation, and then, what subject do you want to talk to me about ?

Helen: thank you dad.

Jack: Thank you uncle, I'm happy to be around but to become happier I want to marry your daughter, and make her my princess.

The uncle: I saw that looks on you two , So Helen is that the man you talked me about?

Helen: yes, dad , he is and I want to marry him too , if you can give us your blessings .

The uncle: I know that my daughter will not choose any man for marriage, of course I will accept it without hesitation.

Jack: Thank you so much ,I'll try all my best to make your daughter happy .

The uncle: son, did you take your parents blessings, I want to know about them too.

Jack: not yet, but they are kind , and a girl like Helen enters immediately to the heart how can my parents don't like her .

The uncle: I will rest assured then.

Jack had known his father well but his mother was not kindhearted or so he thought.....

Helen's Father

Anastasia's real face

Jack went to his home, he did not find anyone or what it looks like...."*Hello, anybody home?*". asked Jack.

_*surprise!!!!* said everyone in the house.

Jack panicked..... It was a party to celebrate Jack's graduation. Everyone was there, his family, friends and neighbours.... After the celebration, the maids cleaned everything and served dinner, the family took their seats.

Jack stood up and said: I want to tell all of you something very important to me.

Jack's father: we are listening son.

Jack: Okay, Dad, I finally found my love, and we decided to get married.

Jack's father: I'm glad to hear that, hoping to see the girl that made you fall in love with her in a short time. **Jack**: my pleasure dad, what do you think mom?

Anastasia looked at her favorite son, so happy, she could not spoil his mood.

Anastasia: of course honey, just do as your father said, I'm sure that she is a good girl.

Anastasia could not take it, her heart broke, because of the news, it was bad news for her.

-*"I feel so tired, I think I will go to sleep, everyone enjoy your dinner and your talk".said Anastasia*

-*"I hope there is nothing bad, sleep well honey".* replied Jack's father.

Jack felt that the news did not please his mom, so he wanted to check out about it. Jack went to his mom's room , he heard her crying..

"mom am I allowed to come in, are you okay?"

Anastasia: yes, you are son, come in *(wiping tears)*

Jack: thank you, mom why are you crying? you know I can't take that, I hope these are tears of joy.

Anastasia: yes, yes they are, I'm very proud of you, you know that you are my favorite son.

Jack: you know that I love you so much, look I will not change after marriage, nobody can take your place and I will never love someone as you .

Anastasia: see, why you are my favorite son, nobody loves me as you do, come here and give your mom a big hug .

Moms can do anything to keep their sons close as much as possible to them.

After this warm conversation, the lady did not change her mind, she did not want her son to get married. Even though she knew her son very well, that he would never change, she thought of a way to take this girl away, even if it takes to kill this innocent girl !!

Anastasia will apply her idea in the appropriate time.

Everyone had a calm night , except Jack , he got a weird feeling after Astastasia's talk,*"Maybe I exaggerate, any mom can react like that or more, if she hears her son   will get married. It was a long day I should sleep".*

In the early morning, Anastasia went to the kitchen. *"Shoshanna called Patrick (the guardian) for me"*

They went to a secret room in the house..

Anastasia: I want you to do me a favor and I can't trust anyone except you.

Patrick: yes, madam anything you want.

Anastasia: Jack, want to get married to a young girl , but I can't accept that , I want you to finish her for me, when I give you the sign to do that.

Patrick: count it as it happened Madam.

The Explosion Truth

Jack went to Helen's home to take her to see his parents ,he wanted to surprise them .

Helen: Jack , what if your parents did not like me?

Jack: what? Why are you asking such a question?

Helen: I don't know, I just had a bad feeling about it.

Jack had the same feeling too, he does not know his mom's reaction after that night .

Jack: Look Helen you know that I love you as you are and nothing will change that.

Helen: yes, I know, I love you too .

Jack: *(kissed her forehead)*we are almost there.

Five pm coffee time for lady Anastasia.... taking a seat and drinking her coffee in a satisfied way while thinking of a way to finish the poor Helen.

Shoshanna went to open the door.

Shoshanna: welcome Master , My lady.

Anastasia: my lady ? who?Hello dear ....she must be the girl you talked to us about ,what a pretty lady!

welcome my daughter Act like you are in your house. Jack felt so relieved After that.

Jack: yes, mother this is my woman.

Anastasia: what's your name darling?

Helen: He.... Helen Madam.

Anastasia: what a beautiful name, please don't call me Madam, call me mom my dear, Shoshanna prepare a special meal for our special guest.

Shoshanna: yes, ma'am.

The three spent a great time talking and laughing for hours … Anastasia liked the girl, she had all that it is required for a noble lady, but she did not want that feeling to control her to change her mind.

Days had passed , All the family liked Helen and Helen had the same feelings, Jack was so happy because his wedding date had approached. Unfortunately, that day did not reach……

One day, the poor Helen came to visit Jack and his family .

-*"Helen come my dear I was waiting for you"*.

said Anastasia

Helen: Thank you , mom.

Anastasia: I have daughters but I feel like you're the closest one to my heart, so I wanted to give you my wedding dress, *(tears dropping)*, come with me .

Helen: Oh mom ,you are so nice to me , you know ,I lost my mom when I was a little girl but thanks to God , he gives me one.

Anastasia took Helen to her room …" *Here, my daughter, try this dress, I will let you try it and I'll go to see if Shoshanna needs help"* Anastasia went to the kitchen, *"Shoshanna call Patrick for me"*.

Anastasia: Patrick the right time is now go and do your job before somebody comes.

Patrick : yes, madam, right now.

Patrick went to the room, he found Helen in a deep   sleep, he tipped her mouth and tied her with a rope tightly, Helen woke up in panic and did not understand what was going on …

"just follow me for your all good" said Patrick.

Patrick took Helen to the woods and let her free; he could not kill her as Anastasia ordered .

Patrick: Please, lady Helen forgive me. I just did what Madam told me to do .

Helen: who ? lady Anastasia , oh my god , she wanted to kill me? What did I do?

Patrick: Yes, I don't know, Miss Helen for your good you must disappear from here if you need any help just let me know .

Helen: I appreciate your kindness Patrick , I really do.

Patrick: Now go faster before anyone sees us .

Helen ran as fast as she could , finally she arrived at her house .

Helen: Dad open the door! , open the door!, come on. **Helen's father**: I'm coming dear, take it easy.

Helen: Ohh! dad *(crying so hard)*, I just can't believe what happened today, I just survived from death.

Helen's father: what are you talking about? What happened Helen?

Helen: We must go somewhere , disappear from here , let's prepare our suits and I will explain to you everything in our way.

Patrick went to the Lady and told her that the mission is done, Anastasia knew that she counted on the right person.

All the memories are confronting in Jack's head...

"Helen I just want to know, where did you go without saying any word, you did love me right? How could you break my heart for years Helen? I hope to meet you soon and hear from you the full story".

jack arrived home ....

Shoshanna: welcome home Master , do you want me to prepare something for you?

Jack: No, thank you, I just want to know where is mom.

Shoshanna: I did not see your mom, the whole day, since she went to your dad's room.

Jack: Okay , I'll go there, Shoshanna please take a rest. **Shoshanna**: *(master is really a kind person)*, I will.

Jack went upstairs , he was about to knock on the door but he heard a loud voice, like his mom and his dad were arguing *."Anastasia why you're screaming my dear , I can hear you , why you are heartless you want me to die soon, all has the right to take his part from the heritage, you can't stop this, please."*said Jack's father.

Anastasia: of course , I just want to protect my son's wealth form his siblings, they don't deserve anything, I protected Jack from his siblings evil , like I did with Helen's .

Jack's father: what, Helen? What did you do to the poor girl , oh God , she was such a noble girl , such a pure one , oh my god I can't take it .... my heart is hurting me.

Anastasia: No , she was not , I killed her with my hands , I only know my son's benefits.

Jack's father: Anastasia, you're a crazy woman, how could you kill an innocent person oh God, I can't take it *(crying so hard)*.

Gustave Stone

Gustave's Funeral

"Anastasia , I can't take it , I can't believe that I married a devil, oh God my heart will stop!".

Anastasia: I only did that for my beloved Jack.

Anastasia opens the door ...

Honey you are here, my son, I was waiting for you all day..why you're looking at me like this *(I hope that he did not hear anything)*.

Jack: mom please tell me that what I heard is a lie, please.

Anastasia: my dear I saw evil in Helen's eyes, she only wanted you because you are rich, believe me.

Jack: I'm sure that Helen is not that kind of person but mom killing her, is something that I did not expect it from you.!!

Jack entered in anger to the room.

Jack: daaaaad, dad please speak, say something.

Jack's father: ja ja ...Jack my son, I think this is my time.

Jack: Dad, please don't say that, no it's not, no it's not *(crying in suffering)*.

Jack's father: please take care of your mother and I want to see your siblings for the last time ...

Anastasia: Finally this old man will let me in peace. **Jack**: can't you hear that, My dad will die, and he wants to see my siblings (sob, sob ,sob).

Anastasia: *(Never, they will take all the money)*, okay, I will send Patrick to call them....

Jack: Mom, daddy is dead, he is gone ..

Everyone in the house was so sad for losing Gustave, Jack's father, he was a great husband and a great father but Anastasia did not deserve him.

Today is Gustave's funeral, everyone was there to farewell this great man, while everybody was in deep sadness, heartbroken, Anastasia was in an extra happiness. After days of this horrible event, Jack did not talk to his mom for a while, he did not want to stop talking to her but he just needed time to realize what happened, However, Anastasia did not care much for that, she just cared for the money. Jack felt like he lived suffering for the first time, which reminded him About little Marie.

losing someone, it's a horrible thing especially your parents and if that parent was the great one.

Jack met Daniel .....

Jack: really it was a great thing to meet you that day, thanks to God I met a great friend.

Daniel: what is happening with you, you look miserable.

Jack : I just lost my Dad (get emotioned).

Daniel: Oh God! Sorry for your loss my friend.

Jack: And I am really shocked by Mom!! I did not expect All that evil inside her!

Daniel: what? What happened Jack?

Jack: Can you believe that my mom killed my first love and because of her dad died .

Daniel: killed her, I can not believe it ! poor Helen she was a great girl.

Jack: I did not believe it either , but I don't know why I always feel that Helen is still alive , I feel it deeply.

Daniel: who knows, maybe because she's really still alive, sometimes the feelings go right, especially lovers feelings.

After Gustave's funeral, Jack did not like to stay at home so he asked Daniel if he could stay with him . Daniel accepted without thinking and he was so excited about it. Jack went to his house to take his belongings,

Anastasia was waiting for him, she started to feel alone.

Anastasia: Jack you're finally here, Jack where are you going? talk to me please , you will know the benefit for what I did later*(in anger)*.

Jack: mom please...I'll move out for a while , I really need time with myself.

Anastasia: as you wish, as you wish Jack. *(I did the impossible for*

your own benefit and this is the way you treat me), sigh ,Jack do you have a place to stay in ?

Jack: don't worry about me, mom.

Jack felt guilty because he will let his mom alone, anyone in his place ,this is the least thing he will do. Jack went to Shoshanna and asked her to take good care of his mom . Before Jack went out , Patrick called him.

Patrick: Sir, I want to talk with you about something . **Jack**: Yes, Patrick what do you want ?

Patrick: I can't live with this secret anymore let's go somewhere , I can't tell it here .

Jack: Patrick, you scared me out , okay let's go ……now tell me .

Patrick: Okay , firstly your wife , I mean Helen is alive and sorry to tell you …

Jack: what?, but mom killed her personally, how could you know that?

Patrick: Sir, I know that because your mom ordered me to do it ,I took her to the woods and let her free but unfortunately, I don't know her place..

Jack: Patrick thank you so much for this good news .

no body can't hide feelings , especially people who have pure hearts ..

Anastasia noticed happiness on Jack's face *"what's made him so happy in sudden"*.

Jack had gone to Daniel's house…. the dinner was on the table, and it looked delicious..

Daniel: It's a good feeling ,when someone comes and cuts the loneliness in this place.

Jack: I really need a warm place to stay in, I don't feel that in my house anymore... I forgot to tell you ,a man working in my house told me that Helen is still alive! **Daniel**: Oh really! , glad to know that , really it's a good news .

Jack: yes, this news revives my heart , thank God.

Helen is still alive and she started work as a teacher for high studies, she has to come back to her hometown because she gave free courses every week in one of the universities there and she hope to meet Jack, maybe she can make the things clear between them .

I want to say to all people who lost their parents or one of them or anyone so precious in childhood or adulthood that they are in a good place ,as always you're alive do good duties that will make them happy.

Anastasia's Regret

early morning….. Daniel got ready to go to the University, Jack wanted to go with him for a change, he missed college days…

Jack: You did not tell me that you're a teacher in the university, which we graduated from, really it was good days.

Daniel: We were good friends the three of us : me ,you and Helen.

Jack: yeah, I hope Helen was between us today .

….Helen was there indeed, giving her free courses in the university .

Daniel went to start his session and let Jack take a round in the university.

Jack was crossing by one class over there and he heard a voice similar to Helen's. He was stunned for a while and said: " *unbelievable, she could not be her*".

Helen went out the opposite door, Jack got in but he did not find her ,"*maybe, it was a coincidence*". the students were still in there so he asked one of those students.

Jack: Hello son, can I ask you a question?

The student: Hello sir, yes sure.

Jack: Who is the teacher that was giving courses just now?

The student: she is not an official teacher here but she came one time in week to give free courses , her name is Helen but I don't re-member her last name, is there any problem?

Jack: No, I'm just asking, thank you son , thank you very much *(she had the same name , the same voice is this a coincidence or it's really her?)*.

Daniel: Hey ,you are here, why do you look like you heard some-thing unusual?

Jack: Nothing , there is nothing don't worry my friend. Daniel finished his session, they went home together for lunch, They started chatting and telling their stories, Daniel asked Jack why he had traveled to that town... Jack replied to him that in the beginning he went there only for calm and peace but he stayed there because there was something that attracted him deeply. while talking, Jack missed little Marie so much, *"what's going on right now with her?"*.

Daniel finished eating and came back to the university for the afternoon session. While Jack stayed at home, he wanted to read some books in Daniel's library,

He started to read a historical book, the book was interesting enough to take Jack away, Jack wanted to come back to the town so badly but he needed to know more that can help him to save little Marie, Jack continues reading until he falls asleep. The win-dow opened in sudden , little Marie entered the room, standing in front of Jack, *"how I miss to look at you, I miss your being around , please return to the castle"*. Jack woke up and he could not believe his eyes ,*"little Marie is that really you?"*

little Marie: yes, it's me Jack ,why you stayed here for a long time?

Jack: It happened a lot of events , bad events, that's why I could not come .

little Marie: sorry, to hear that, but I hope that you come soon, you know that I don't feel secure unless you are around.

Jack: I know that very well, little Marie I need more information to keep my promise, when I'll find more clues , I'll come back there, I'll try to make it faster.

little Marie: I never believed in someone, but you, I believe anything you say.

little Marie transformed to a dust and disappeared , Jack had some joy when he finally saw little Marie in a "good health", the joy will complete when Jack finds the truth. Jack wanted to visit his mom, Although she hurt him so deeply ,He decided to forgive her. She still his mom nothing will change, he wants to go to his house to know the full truth from his mom's mouth.

Anastasia finally get that money nothing comes before family ,she felt guilty for anything she done , she wanted to change to a good person and forget her bad side forever," ohh, God please forgive me , I killed my husband , my great husband, I disjoint the family , I hurt my favorite son , only for what , only for the wealth, if he did not forgive me, he has the right but I wish that from my heart "*(crying so hard).*

Shoshanna came to the room running *" madam , what happened to you, is everything all right?*

Anastasia: Oh my daughter, I have always been so mean to you please forgive me, come here , come here. **Shoshanna**: *(is madam all right? she looks different),* Okay, Madame I forgive you ,stop crying.

Anastasia: I hope that my husband and my kids do the same.

Shoshanna: I'm sure that sir Jack will forgive you. He had a pure heart and for Sir Gustave he already did before dying, I'm certain about that.

Anastasia: Really? how did you know that?

Shoshanna: one day I was serving sir Gustave dinner, he gave me this letter, he told me to give it to you in the right time, so I think this is the right time... I'll let you read it, I'm going to make some coffee for you, I'll take my leave ma'am.

Anastasia: thank you ,come here Shoshanna (gave her a strong hug).

Anastasia took a seat and started reading the letter, Gustave considered her as a good wife although her mistakes, *"Anastasia my first love and my last one , as you know I have a dangerous disease and I feel that I will die soon , I give the wealth to you , I know that behind all this cruelty , there is a white side ,I know that you will use it wisely, I write this letter to you because I want to tell you that I forgive you for anything and I hope that you forgive me if I did something wrong to you without knowing.... from your first love... Gustave"*. Anastasia got emotional and surprised because of the letter and promised Gustave that she will use the wealth wisely, and she will be a different person from now on," *thank you Gustave for everything you always make me happy even in your death"*

Shoshanna: Madam, come on down , there is someone wants to see you .

Patrick the loyal man

Family Reunification

Shoshanna: Madam, there is someone who wants to see you.

Anastasia: Shoshanna okay, I'm coming (*I hope that someone is Jack*).

Jack goes upstairs...

Jack: mom, I missed you a lot.

Anastasia: Jack, is that really you, I missed you so much, so much.

Jack hugged his mom tightly, and they went downstairs holding their hands. they took their seats and drank coffee...

Jack: Mom,I came here to tell you that I forgive you about everything you did because I know that you're a good person, somehow, and I really need to know the full story please.

Anastasia: okay, my son ,I'll tell you everything, Shoshanna my daughter please call Patrick and come to join us .

Shoshanna: yes, madam.

Anastasia: since we are all here, then , I'll talk, Jack I know that you are looked at me in a low way , but to be honest with you I loved the girl you chose , I really did ,but the ambition got inside my heart, One day Helen came to visit us, no one was here except me Patrick and Shoshanna, I welcomed her and I wanted to give her my wedding dress as a gift and made her closer to me ,When she went to my room to try the dress we had an emotional chat ,I really meant those words and considered her as a real daughter for me but now and I'm imaging all those bad things I done, oh God , I feel that I'm really an evil, Then Helen was so satisfied with the dress I let her to try it after that I went downstairs to call Patrick to kidnap her and throw her in the woods after killing her.... but please Jack don't blame Patrick he just followed my orders and I promise you that I'll change to a good person.

Jack: I know that ,because I know what happened after that , I mean what really happened.

Anastasia: How did you know that?

Jack: Patrick told me the full story, and Patrick is a real good man, because he did not follow all your orders , Helen is still alive.

Anastasia:Oh really ! you did the good Patrick.

Patrick: Thank you, madam.

Anastasia: thank you for not following my order, you saved a life.

Jack: yes, he did.

Anastasia felt so relief after telling everything, they enjoyed their coffee together, Anastasia decided to care about Shoshanna as her daughter by made her a free slave, Shoshanna felt so happy for that and accepted Anastasia as a mother, she did not want to go anywhere , in the end it is her home too.

Anastasia: Jack I want to talk with you about something , let's go upstairs.

Jack: okay, mom.

Anastasia: take a seat my dear son.... as you know your father left us a huge wealth and your siblings have the right in it too, so I want you to call them for that and discuss it as a family.

Jack: I know that,(*it seems that something happened, let mom think that way)*, yes it's the right thing to do .

Anastasia: you know , your dad thought that was the right thing to do too (*feeling so sad)*.

Jack: How did you know that?

Anastasia: Well, your dad before dying ,he wrote to me a letter, a forgiveness letter , Shoshanna showed it to me a couple hours ago.....here ,it is Jack.

Jack: Mom ,I always knew that dad is a kind man , now let's do what we should do in the beginning.

Even if Gustave told Jack that he will give him the heritage , he wants his mom to have it all, and he knew that his dad always does the right thing .

Jack brings his siblings. After they arrived The atmosphere between them was emotional, hate , anger.. but in the end it get calm and everyone went to the cemetery to visit Gustave's grave , they hugged each other tightly , and cried so hard.

of course losing a parent it's not easy especially when you did not know on time. Anastasia has the responsability of everything happened she asked forgiveness from her kids and promised them that everything will change from now on ... they had dinner , in home like a family again , everyone decided to throw anything bad from the past out and live a peaceful happy life ..

Anastasia felt completely satisfied and happy, she finally saw her kids around.

Anastasia: Jack ,thank you so much ,I always know that you are special , thanks to God that he gives me a son like you.

Jack: I'm thankful for being my mom too.

everyone spent a warm and a clam night , Jack could not sleep ,so he got out ..." *If I find Helen again ,will she accept to come back to me? will she trust me and my family again?...Helen it's a good woman but what she lived is hard , I hope she can forgive mom*"

Helen in her house looking from the window to the sky "*I wonder if Jack still remember me...PFF, how's that and I'm not an outstanding woman to them!*"

Helen's father hated the stone's family because they did not accept his daughter without any reason ."*Helen sweetheart what's makes you a wake in such time , go and get some rest*"

Helen after escaping to another city, she found difficulty to get familiar to the place , difficulty to find a job , she had to work scaly jobs for couple cents and they passed some days without eating ,but now, everything changed to good , Helen was a patient girl , she never had complained , she believed deeply that everything will change to the best. For all what she did to make her father happy and proud, he wanted Helen to get married and have her own family ,someone who really deserves his own daughter, he decided to talk about that later .

Helen lying on her bed , thinking of Jack if he really forgot her and got married to another woman, *"Oh my God ,am I still loving him? Jack did not do anything wrong to me, everything was done by his mother "* even though Helen still loves Jack but she needs to convince her father first.

In this chapter we lived a lot of emotional events and we learned that everyone deserves a chance so let's be more tolerant and kind.

Daniel the Good Friend

Jack took his breakfast with his family then he went to Daniel , he just went without letting him know, luckily Daniel had a day off. Jack knocked on the door, but no one was responding
.... A few minutes later,

Daniel: Ohh, Jack what are you doing here so early? **Jack**: So sorry, to disturb you in the early morning.

Daniel: It's okay ,today is my day off, I just prepared breakfast, by the way , where have you been? you just went without saying anything!

Jack: yeah, about that ..

Daniel: excuse me ... Let's go inside and finish our talk while eating breakfast.

Daniel and Jack took their seats and started talking.. **Daniel**: Alright, now we can talk in relief , jack join me to breakfast , we are friends I don't need to ask you that.

Jack: Okay, well, I just had my breakfast at home.

Daniel: really ? Good to hear that you finally joined your family.

Jack: I'm glad too, well, I forgave mom and she promised me that she will change , I'm hoping that she is telling the truth.

Daniel: Just to say that it requires courage, for me just believe her even though it's hard.

Jack: Yes, that's what I decided, anyway, when I went home I found my mom miserable, after a long conversation she told me the full story , and I'm glad that she did not kill Helen.

Daniel: That's good then, The guardian was saying the truth.

Jack: Yes, but I need to know where is she? and you're the person who can help me with that.

Daniel: me? How is that?

Jack: do you remember the day ,when we were in the university , and you asked what's wrong with me.

Daniel: yes , I do , what's the link?

Jack: When I crossed by a classroom there, I heard Helen's voice and what was surprising is that the teacher has the same name , I don't think that is a coincidence ,what do you think?

Daniel: well, maybe she is really Helen maybe not , So I can understand that you want me to search for her there , it's kind of hard because of the University rules, but I'll do my best.

Jack: Daniel what would 1 do without you? God bless you my friend!

Daniel: Please, Jack if I were in your place , I'm sure you will do the same or more.

Jack: of course.

Daniel and Jack spent all the day together around the city, they had a great time, *"I really needed to go out with someone, when I was alone ,I was spending my days at home reading and teaching in the university,I did not have friends to spend time with"*. Said Daniel. After a long day outside, Jack and Daniel went to bed early. Jack looked through the window ,looking at the sky full of stars,*"I hope that Helen still loves me, I can't wait to meet her again"*.

Helen was looking in the sky at the same time as Jack...

-*"Helen come here my daughter, come and have dinner with your father"*

-*"I'm coming Dad"*

Helen's father did not know from where he will start the subject.

-*"My Helen look at you how beautiful you are, you should look for a husband, I don't want to see my daughter live Alone"*

-*"Oh! dad come on , I'm not alone , I have you"*

-*"Okay, I just want you to be happy that's all"*

Helen Hold her father's hand.." *I know, I know, but dad, I'm really happy this way"*. Helen cleaned the dishes and went to her room , lying on the be*d "Oh, Jack it's obvious that I still love you but I think that we aren't a match"*.

Beautiful weather, trees are blooming , it's the spring season and it seems that it will bloom for the stone family too.

Daniel went to the university whistling, he had a feeling that today is a different day somehow

..... He entered to the university, luckily nobody notice his existence and he start searching file after file.... a few minutes after, the surprise was that the girl was Helen, *"Oh, my god it is Helen for real"*, Daniel start writing the information faster on a paper.

  .....After he finished his session, he resort to his house. *"Jack ,open ,open...come on!"*

Jack: coming...coming, Daniel, what happened?

Daniel: it was her, Helen is that teacher in the University.

Jack: Oh! really ? What good news! Thank you so much for your help *(hugging Daniel tightly)*

Now everything has shown up but will Helen and Jack return to each other?

Helen is a good girl and kind hearted, but what happened to her was not easy to forget.

... -*"Helen be quick my daughter, you will be late for your work"*.

-*"Don't worry dad , I won't"*, Helen kissed her dad and got out in a hurry .

Today Helen went to the university and started her course as usual, the classroom was unusual full, every student there likes Helen's way of teaching in addition to the free courses ,Jack joined the classroom without Helen noticed ,*"I always known that you'll be a great teacher ever, here I am watching you doing your great Job "*. Helen finished her session, everyone in the class stood around her, they wanted answers for their questions, Jack wanted to take the chance and went there too. *"Okay , okay haha, I'll try to answer some of your questions and let the rest for the next session. Are we okay?"* Said Helen, -" Okay, teacher".

After a couple of minutes Helen finished answering the questions and started work on something.

Jack: teacher , I have a question please?

Helen: *(this voice seems familiar)*, Yes, ask anything you want *(concentrated on her work)*.

Jack: I want you to forgive me .

Helen: What ! Ja... Jack , Jack what are you doing here? everything between us was done a long time ago, I don't want to talk with you!

Jack: I know , you are so angry you have the right to be , but give me a chance , I did not know all that happened to you , I just found out recently.

Helen: Okay, but that doesn't change anything, I really need time to think and dad will not accept our wedding anyway.

Jack: Okay, I'll give you time, Helen. I really was in need of you a couple days ago .

Helen: Why ?What happened in those days?

Jack: We recently finished preparation for my dad's funeral and I stopped talking with mom for a while but now everything is okay. The great thing that happened those days is that I met Daniel, and he really stood for me.

Helen: Oh! , really it happened a lot , I'm really sorry for your loss, uncle Gustave was a great man unlike aunt Anastasia, anyway, I'm glad that you met our friend Daniel.

Jack: thank you, Helen , I'm really still in love with you, I hope you are too.

Helen: Jack , I have to go.

Jack: Okay, I will not take more of your time .

Helen collected her stuff and went out , Jack decided to follow her, he wanted to know her address, *"noway Helen , I won't lose you anymore , I can't live without you"*.

Helen's Showing Up

Jack took the car and started following the cab. He just wants to get familiar with the way, he stands a little far to not be noticed. Jack returns to Daniel's house

Jack: Daniel, today I met Helen and we had a short conversation, although it seems that she doesn't want to marry anymore but I have feelings that she still loves me.

Daniel: That's good, but I think that you should give her time, don't take things in a hurry.

Jack: Yes, you are right let's go out and have lunch.

Daniel: since you will pay for it I'm in haha.

Helen prepared lunch and called her father. They started eating in a silence until….

" Dad , what if I met Jack again , will you talk to him?"

-" Why such a question? You already know the answer."

-" Okay, dad but what if he had no relation with what happened to me because he was not there".

-" well, I don't know, Jack is a good man but I still need time to decide ".

-" Okay, dad"

-" why do you ask that ? did you meet him?"

-" No, dad I did not"

-" well, finish your meal and take a rest, you must feel exhausted after your long day".

-*"Okay, dad if you need anything just let me know"*

Helen wanted to give another chance to Jack but not so quick, she needs time to do that, especially that lady Anastasia it's a hard woman to deal with.

All the past days were happy days for everyone except for Natalie the wife of Jack's neighbour even though it was not a good lady ,but the poor woman , she lost her husband.

In the early morning policemen knocked on Natalie's door

-*" Good morning , Madam "*

-*" Good morning , sir (with a shaking voice).*

"Does Jerry Rosbon have any relation with you?"

-*"yes, he is my husband , why? is there anything wrong?"*

-*"yes, Actually, I'm really sorry, I'm sorry for your loss madam"*

-*" what? Are you sure that is him?"*

-*" he is now in the dead refrigerator, you can check that if you want to, we found him dead in the road and we found those papers. Ma'am!, ma'am!, take it easy"*

After this shock news Natalie passed out the policemen took her inside and put her on the couch after a couple of minutes, Natalie woke up and found her friend

beside her *"Oh, Natalie you're finally awake"*

-*"Oh, God ,my head hurting me so much ....(start*

crying)"

 -*"Oh, come here my dear, I know how you're feeling"*. After the situation calmed down, Natalie and her friend went together to check the body

...When Natalie saw her husband's body, she could not hold on , her friend accompanied her to home and took very good care of her . After a couple of days, Natalie wanted to tell Jack about her husband. He has the right to know about him ,they were friends,

Natalie asked her friend to write a letter to Jack.

Jack went to visit his mom, but no one was home, even Shoshanna and Patrick. The mailbox was full of mails, Jack took those mails and read the addresses, *"is this the countryside's address?"*, *"I hope there is nothing wrong"*. He opened the enveloppe

 Jack read the letter and he was shocked, he took a paper and wrote to his mom that he will go to the countryside accompanied with his friend Daniel

... -"Daniel, I need you to do another favor for me."

-"yes, sure as always I could ."

-"I want you to go with me to the countryside."

-"Yes there is no problem , it's holiday time anyway , but why do you want to travel there? Is there something bad?"

-"Yes, I lost another close person!"

-"Oh! so sorry to hear that!"

After they got ready, Jack and Daniel went to the train station.Couple of hours later they finally arrived, Jack did not want Daniel to come with him only for this reason, he wanted him to meet the little Marie since the castle is so near to Jerry's house. They went to Natalie's house for condoling and to see if she needs help.

Jerry Rosbon

Another Chance

Natalie thanked Jack for his care and asked him to stay for dinner but he excused her for leaving.

Jack and Daniel went to the castle to spend the night there, *"Daniel this is the castle that I talked you about, look how much it attracts".* said Jack.

The lights were on, the dinner was served, Daniel was surprised *"you were living here alone right?".*

-*"kind of, let's have dinner then I'll explain to you everything".*

-*"jack please, I want to know first, is this place haunted (body shaking)".* Suddenly little Marie appeared, and said *"is there anything wrong with my welcoming way?".*

-Daniel freaked out "Jack let's get out from here".

-*"Daniel don't be afraid!, it's just a little girl, let's have a seat".*

all the three took their seats ,and started eating.

-*"Jack that's why you went to the library that day, you want to know about the girl's story".*

-*" yes, that's the reason, will you help me with that?"*

-*"yes, of course, the girl does not look harmful at all, she looks innocent".*

little Marie felt so happy for the return of jack and for meeting another kind man, while they were eating ,she was looking at them.

-*"little girl, stop looking and join us, your cook is so delicious".*

-*" I'm glad that you like it".*

Jack and Daniel spent a nice evening in the castle, they decided to search about Marie's story tomorrow.

Helen was thinking about what jack told her that day, *"Actually, he is right , he has nothing to do with what happened to me, maybe I should give him another chance".* she decided to go to Jack's house to give him another opportunity but she was not sure if Anastasia will allow that.

Helen woke up early in the morning and made breakfast for her father and she took her way to Jack's house . After couple of hours Helen arrived at the house, and rang the bell.

Anastasia asked Shoshanna to open the door.. **Shoshanna** :" lady Helen! please come in"

Helen: it's okay Shoshanna , I want to see Jack. **Shoshanna**: my lady, Jack is not here.

Anastasia stood...

 Anastasia : Shoshanna my dear ,what makes you take all this time....oh Helen! come in my dear please.

Helen: Okay, Shoshanna, so I take my leave .

Anastasia: please Helen, I want to talk to you.

A sudden silence covered the atmosphere.

Helen: okay, let's talk here .

Anastasia: I beg you , come inside and join us for breakfast.

Helen: Alright.(*thinking about it*).

Anastasia admitted all her bad things that she did in the past ,and asked forgiveness from Helen.

Anastasia: Helen, believe me I really liked you but the ambition made me blind, I really want you to forgive me.

Helen:Lady Anastasia, what you commit made me live a tough life, and my dad hated you a lot, but even if that takes time to cure, I'll forgive you after all.

Anastasia:Oh Helen!, thank you so much my dear, Jack was completely right about you (*hugged her tightly*). Even if forgiveness was a hard decision for Helen but

she felt that she did the right thing.

forgiveness is able to create new people, to cure wounds and even save lives please let it be one of your principes in your life :)

Marie's Freedom

For the first time after a long period, Finally it showed up the right man to reveal the truth of the mysterious castle .

Jack did not go to the countryside library in the first place because he thought that the librarian would consider him insane, but all what happened to little Marie and his meeting with Daniel let him make this decision. Jack and Daniel went to the library hoping to find something there, even if the library was an old and abandoned place, However it contained many interesting books, The librarian joined Jack and Daniel..

The librarian: Good morning gentlemen, How can I help you?

Daniel: Good morning,sir.

Jack: Good morning sir, well, I lived in the castle for a long time, it happened to me several weird things, so I'm here to know about the story of the castle.

The librarian: you're in the right place. the castle has a very old story, A long time ago the Royal family was living there, the dynasties after had disappeared from the castle because of a ghost of a little girl, they were Waking every night in her hard screaming, the lights were on by themselves and the sounds of broken dishes were so annoying and a lot of other scary things.

Jack was surprised and said ,*"from where did you know this story?"*.

The librarian: when the castle got abandoned, I entered and took some books from there, then, I came to the library and examined them. The story I just told you, I read it from one of those books, hold on , I'll bring it for you.

Jack: thank you, sir.

Jack and Daniel flipped the book's papers, they found the missing pages of the book was in the castle .*"Little Marie was a daughter of a slave there, the butler was so tough with her by giving her hard duties to do, when Marie got tired ,she was taking her toys and her books with her near to the bridge, and started playing and running around the field. One day the butler was calling her, but she didn't respond , the butler went to the field and she found the little girl playing there, she started screaming at her and hitting her so hard, then she drowned her in the lake untill she died"*. Jack felt so sad when he knew about the little Marie's story and he wanted to think of a way to make Marie free again.

Helen was missing Jack and she could not wait to meet him again, at that day Anastasia told Helen that Jack is in the countryside - she knew that from a note there- in case she thought to return to him.

Helen decided to go and meet him....

-*" Dad can I talk to you about something?"*

-*"yes, dear, go ahead"*.

"dad, please promise me that you will not get mad first."

-*"okay, I promise"*.

-*"I went to Jack's home to understand what's really happened, but I did not find him and I found Anastasia, she asked for forgiveness and she told me that Jack had no relation with what she planned, it was really hard for me to forgive her even though I did"*.

-*"Alright, you went there without permission, so what is your request now?"*.

-*"dad, please don't make it hard for me, I just want you to forgive them like I did. and I really want to become Jack's wife".*

-"so, that what you want to ask, you know that to forgive Anastasia is a hard thing for me, but I can't refuse any request of you, you are my precious daughter, I'll try that".

- "Oh! thank you dad".

Jack thought for a great idea to save little Marie and was sure that the field was the clue , he asked Daniel to buy a variety of plants to plant them in the field and he asked for everyone's help.

∞∞∞∞

Helen decided to take the way to the countryside, and now all the problems between the two families had been solved, Helen asked her dad, Anastasia ,and Shoshanna to go with her.

Finally the waiting day had come.

.... Helen and the others had arrived to the countryside, the castle is in the center of the area, Jack noticed his family from there and he went to welcome them...

-"Helen, what happened, why everybody is here".

-"Jack,I'm here to give you another chance, your mother clarified everything to me".

Jack hugged her and welcomed his family to the castle.

- "mom, it's really a good surprise, I'm happy that all of you are here".

Jack felt so happy, he is finally with Helen, and they will get Married sooner, but still one thing is missing for this happiness to be completed..

Day after day the plants start growing till the field is back to life again, Jack was waiting for little Marie to come and play in the field like she used to do in the past.

A few days later Jack was looking through the window, he saw little Marie running in the field with full happiness, he ran faster and called her,*"Mariiie, you're here!"*

-*" Thank you Jack , thank you for saving me " (hugging each other)*

-*"I'm finally free, I'm free"*, little Marie flew far away with all the shades were in the castle, they are turning around her until they disappeared. Jack got emotional and started crying *" Goodbye,little Marie, goodbye, I'm glad that I kept my promise".* Jack wanted to keep all that in secret, he felt so happy because little Marie is free after years of suffering....

WEDDING DAY....

Anastasia: Shoshanna my dear ,please take care of the decoration, I'll go to see if Helen wanted some help. **Shoshanna**: Okay, mother. Helen was in the room, wearing the wedding dress, she could not believe that this day is her wedding day.

Anastasia: tok, tok, Helen Am I allowed to come in. **Helen**: yes, of course ,please come in.

-*"Oh look at you ! my beautiful daughter, (crying)".*

-*"Oh come on, you will make me cry too, (get touched)".*

Everyone in the countryside was so happy for Jack's wedding. Today is the day of Helen and Jack, they finally will get married.

Anastasia occupied all the wedding needs ,she wanted it to be the best day ever for Helen and jack.

Jack was in the room with Daniel, waiting for her bride to get ready.

Helen was locked herself in the room she was so nervous.

Anastasia: Helen my dear, are you ready, come on the religious man is here and Jack is waiting for you downstairs.

Helen: O O Okay, I'm coming.

-*"so gorgeous, so beautiful".* said the presence. Helen showed up and her father accompanied her all the way. Jack was stunning in his beautiful bride..

-*"Now, go to your husband, my Beautiful daughter ,Jack, take good care of my daughter, I'm wishing you two a happy life".*

and they lived happily ever after ❤